GOLDEN SHACKLES

Behind Blue Eyes Book 3

SARA J. BERNHARDT

Lavish
Publishing LLC

First Edition

Behind Blue Eyes, book 3

2019 Lavish Publishing, LLC

All Rights Reserved

Published in the United States by Lavish Publishing, LLC, Midland, TX

Cover Design by: Alexcia Productions

Cover Images: CANSTOCK

Paperback Edition

ISBN: 978-1-944985-77-6

www.LavishPublishing.com

Contents

For my Adam

"IN all the darkest pages of the malign supernatural there is no more terrible tradition than that of the Vampire, a pariah even among demons. Foul are his ravages; gruesome and seemingly barbaric are the ancient and approved methods by which folk must rid themselves of this hideous pest. Even to-day in certain quarters of the world, in remoter districts of Europe itself, Transylvania, Slavonia, the isles and mountains of Greece, the peasant will take the law into his own hands and utterly destroy the carrion who--as it is yet firmly believed--at night will issue from his unhallowed grave to spread the infection of vampirism throughout the countryside"

~Montague Summers~

Prologue

IT STARTED IN 5000 B.C., the time that historians call "the time before the pharaoh," when in reality there had been kings of Egypt longer ago than anybody could have believed.

There was a king called Ashman the Great, son of Atares. He was to wed a woman of royal blood.

Ashman had no sisters or cousins to continue his bloodline. He married his brother's daughter, Lanara. There was love between the two, which led to strength and peace in their rule. Lanara was a strikingly beautiful woman with black hair that reached her knees, and her eyes were so deep you could become lost simply by gazing at her.

Ashman wanted an heir to the throne of Egypt and asked the gods for a son. When Queen Lanara gave birth, it was not the son they had hoped for, but a daughter.

With tears and pain, they looked at their child, and Lanara stared into the eyes of her king.

"What has happened?"

The baby princess was small, weak, and it did not appear she would long survive.

The pharaoh knew the people of Egypt could not have a weak woman take the throne. For months they prayed to the gods, begging for the strength of the great kings of old to pass into the weak body of their daughter, but nothing had helped. The life of the princess was fading. The people of Egypt could not know, so the pharaoh and his queen sought care in secret. They set out in the black dead of night to seek a cure for their sick child.

In the times before Ashman, when his father had ruled Egypt, Atares had cast away his advisor Zulous and his wife Deleona from the Kingdom and left them with the fate to dwell forever in the hillsides. They were believed to be sorcerers of great evil and power. Atares feared they would overthrow the Egyptian royal family, so in turn, they were exiled. Ashman felt, however, he had no other choice than to beg for their power. Ashman and Lanara both knew—the payment would not be trivial.

Find the miracle workers they did in the hillsides they had called "the nameless caverns." The people stared silently for a moment at the royalty, wondering why they had come into contact after so many long years. There was a fair-faced man and a lovely black-eyed woman who were both gray in the hair and seemed tired and lonely. The royal ones had even bowed to these strangers, begging for their help.

"Please," Lanara wept. "Can you see she is ill? We've tried everything. We gave to the gods all the offerings that we could."

Lanara sought comfort in her king's embrace as the woman known as Deleona took the baby from her arms.

The sorceress set the squirming infant on a wooden table and stared at her almost in disgust.

"We will offer you any kind of payment you desire. Just please help our child."

Deleona looked into Ashman's eyes and asked quietly. "Anything?"

Ashman nodded. "Anything you ask for."

Deleona and the man known as Zulous had discussed quietly the payment for the child's care. Lanara and Ashman feared what these people sought—whether they would try to take over the throne of Egypt or even harm their princess. Lanara wept again in the arms of Ashman.

The man disappeared for a moment then returned with a bowl of red liquid. He set it beside the baby.

"For the strength we deliver your child, we ask something of you in return," the man started. "Your Majesty, lovely queen, blessed by the gods, if we can make your child fit to rule Egypt, we ask of you a place back in the palace."

"The palace?"

Deleona smiled. "That is what we ask in exchange for this potion of strength we offer your child."

Lanara didn't respond, just looked to Ashman. And so it was that Ashman the Great, the powerful pharaoh dropped his gaze to the floor and fell weak against the strength of his lover's will.

"If it is what you ask for, then your place in our kingdom will be returned, and you will as well be honored with the place of serving our princess as she grows."

"Our thanks to you," Zulous replied, finally bowing to his king and queen.

"We must caution you, however," Deleona started, "that this spell will give Sekhmet intense strength that may cause your people to ask questions."

"But she will live?" Lanara asked.

"She will."

"Then it is worth it. Our departure must be quick. Our people may need us."

Deleona nodded.

They departed back home after baby Sekhmet's ritual, and all they could do was wait for what they hoped would be joyous results.

As time passed, the once dark coal eyes of the princess began to change, and even in shadow, her eyes shone lucent and sparkling amber.

Deleona and Zulous served Sekhmet and grew to love her as their own. She grew into a very beautiful child. In the years to come, the people of Egypt began to talk; even the laboring workers and slaves spoke of Sekhmet, saying she was a powerful sorceress or that she had been blessed by the gods. Some said even—that she herself was divine. Her strength and power could be felt emanating from her very bones.

As Ashman and Lanara grew older, they became desperate to wed their daughter. They arranged a marriage to her cousin, Arole, which was appropriate since he was of royal blood.

Although, if it had been the choice of the princess, a marriage to Arole would not have been the one she would have made. For in secret, there was another, one who shared her strength—a man who called himself Ké Hé Zule, who Sekhmet had met at night when he came to her bedchamber, telling her he had known her his entire life and that it was the will of the gods they be together.

Something more was taking place in the land. Queen Lanara had mysteriously vanished before the very eyes of Ashman. Everywhere, the people talked, they searched, and they mourned. Screams rang through the city night and day. Everywhere people were dying.

"The gods are angry!" Sekhmet said. "They have taken our queen and cursed our lands."

Talk of monsters deep in the sands came to the people of Egypt, and soon they came to believe that Ashman was responsible for this—Ashman, in whose blood ran the power of the gods. Ashman was a cursed man, they said. Only weeks after the disappearance of Lanara, Ashman began to completely ignore the cries of his people and began his life as a nightwalker.

Strange things were happening. The sands of the Sahara were soiled with the corpses of their people, blood stained the golden grounds, and the screams of rage and pain through the lands did not stop.

The once exiled couple who dwelled in the hillsides had taken the princess to her father's bedchamber in the day while he rested.

"Sweet Majesty, do you not see?"

She dropped to her knees to look closer at her sleeping father.

"I do not."

"An accursed man is Ashman," Zulous answered. "A cursed soul he has. The screams at night, Majesty…"

She was instantly horror stricken but could not believe what he was saying. She looked up at Zulous with her striking gold eyes. She looked back down at Ashman and touched his face to smooth his hair upon his forehead.

Deleona covered Sekhmet's mouth before her screams disturbed the pharaoh. They shut the doors of his chambers, and Sekhmet struggled in Zulous's grasp.

"He's cold," she whispered, "frozen cold."

"Cursed," Deleona answered back.

"Dead!" the princess screamed. "Don't you understand? He's dead. The gods have taken my beloved father."

She sank to her knees, covering her face with her hands, choking out her words. "Take him."

"Please, Princess," Zulous begged. "Please listen to us. Your father is not dead. He is cursed. Possessed by our beloved Horus or Osiris sent earthbound to punish us."

"What did he do so terribly wrong?" she wept.

"I only wish I knew," he said. "The gods are angry. They have taken the queen and possessed the body of the pharaoh."

She stared blankly.

As time passed on, the people knew of Ashman's curse but spoke seldom of it.

Sekhmet's marriage to Arole was to become, and on the eve of her unwanted ceremony, something dreadful had happened. The beautiful Princess Sekhmet and the beloved Ashman had vanished from the land, and deep in the sands of Egypt was where Sekhmet dwelled.

"Now, my love," said a soothing voice. "Your cousin Arole will rule Egypt, and you will be my queen, the queen of *my* world."

"Yes, Ké Hé Zule," she said. "Yes, my love. I shall serve you as my master."

There, in the Sahara, Ké Hé Zule fed on the blood of the princess and returned it to her once again, cursing her to thrive forever on the blood of men.

Sekhmet soon came to loathe Ké Hé Zule. She resented him for controlling her. He told Sekhmet she had the power to create others as he had created her. And yet he had forbidden her from doing so. She was a princess after all, and being told she could not create infuriated her.

"I am the father of our kind," he said.

"Then I am the mother."

"You may nurture and care for my children. I alone will be the creator."

The Father stood and watched as his princess discovered her strength and her powers, but all the while, he could read the thoughts of his love as he could others. Her power was too great. He knew not the hatred she felt for him and her plans of his destruction.

Deep in the morning while The Father slept, Sekhmet took a torch to his bed. Before she had time to drop the fire onto his flesh, he sprang toward her, knocking the torch from her hand. Instantly, it became dark as the fire died. He grasped her by the throat.

"Aw, my princess. Such betrayal."

So it was that the father of all that are damned had banished the princess to suffer for all eternity in his chamber of ice hidden deep under the sands of the Arabian Desert.

The years passed on, and The Father was alone again

as he wandered the earth, destroying and creating all in his path.

As the time passed, Sekhmet's strength grew, and she melted that wicked ice and escaped her prison. She searched for her lover and set fire to his flesh. Ké Hé Zule —the father of the damned—was destroyed.

Sekhmet then hid away for centuries, mourning over the pain of all she had lost—and left behind.

Chapter One

NEW HAMPSHIRE.

"The Switzerland of America," with its White Mountains. Ah yes, of all the beauty of this American Switzerland, the White Mountains are the most beautiful thing of all.

The Indians had inhabited these mountains long before the settlement of New England; I myself know how it feels to be forced from a beautiful home. I had come here just to see how much it resembles my Switzerland, and I must say—it does. Its luscious greenery and full, beautiful trees, its gorgeous waters and blue skies, it is my Geneva, as I had always known it. Why don't I ever go back? I am sure you would like to know. Too many memories. I am immortal now. Returning would only confuse me and make me miss Mary and Madeline so miserably that I may weep for days.

California is my home now, and I moved through the night from the peaks of the White Mountains to the cozy blankets of my bed in Moonlight Manor.

I was on my way to see Clem, who lived in a small apartment flat just blocks away. Oh how I loved him. How I loved to simply watch him nibble at his food and sip at his wine. He never got even near drunk, which is something I admired about Clement.

"Are you all right?" he asked me.

I couldn't help but smile at the sound of his beautiful Irish accent. "Yes," I answered. "I am painfully hungry."

"You promised to stay a while," he said in a childish tone.

"A while longer."

"How much longer?"

"Half an hour longer."

"What time is it now?"

"I have no idea," I answered soberly.

"You can look."

"I refuse to look," I demanded.

The thought of time aggravated me. We have and need no concept of time. Of course, I could not focus on such feelings or I could shatter all the clocks in the house. I changed the subject, trying to get to the real reason I had come to see Clem.

"You said you didn't want it from me," I started, "but you did want it."

"Oh, stop it, Adam," he yelled. "You know damn well I didn't mean that. I have explained this to you before. I was under your charm, and it seemed like a good idea at the time."

I took one long stride toward him, wrapping him in an embrace. "Take it, Clem," I said, moving my lips across his ear as I spoke. "Take it."

I felt him shudder, but I wasn't sure what it meant.

"Let me release my power into your body, such a fragile shell."

He shuddered again and let out a long sigh. My voice was becoming softer, and I was unsure if he could even hear me.

"Yes," I whispered. "Yes, take it, my child."

So close. So close I could feel him giving in, I could feel him weaken, surrender. "You want it, my child, my Clem. Take it now—take the blood."

He took a step back. "No," he whispered. But he was calm; he was sorry. "I can't take it."

Of course, how foolish of me to have used the word *blood* when speaking to him, when seducing him with my power. I was so close. How could I have spoken that hated word?

"It's a gift," I said, "and I offer it to you."

"And I decline from your offer. I love you, Adam. You know this. But I don't want to become you. Please, Adam—leave now."

I sighed. "I will leave, Clem. It's been a half an hour by now. Farewell."

He didn't respond.

I returned home to see Relone was there.

"It doesn't matter, Adam," he whispered. "Clem, I mean."

"Oh, I know, Relone. I just thought—I don't know what I thought. Maybe I just thought it would be fun."

He whispered something in French, but I don't know what he said.

"Yes." He laughed. "You are really something. You know that?"

I smiled. *I am Adam Gold. How could Clem resist me?*

I awoke from the feeling of warmth, but it was a comforting feeling, like sitting in front of the fireplace with Mary on Christmas Eve as we decorated the tree, and I smiled.

I opened my eyes and saw the warmth was the sun. The curtains were open. Normally, the sun even through the window hurts my skin, but it didn't. I touched the glass. It was hot, but there was no pain. I had an urging desire to fling open that window. I did. Still there was no pain. I stuck my head out the window, almost plummeting. I could see blue skies and white clouds. The trees were even more beautiful in the daylight, the flowers and the grass. It was a miracle.

Suddenly, I came to myself, and I felt the pain. I had been dreaming, but I realized the curtains really were open, and even though the crystals in the glass broke up the light, I was in pain. I closed the curtains and went back to sleep. I wished I really could walk about in the sunlight, feeling the warmth on my back, seeing my white skin become browned by the light. Our greatest desire is to become human. Can you ask any less of me? Vampires don't feel temperature as intensely as humans. In fact, my teeth haven't chattered in over two centuries. Oh, to be human…what a desire I ache for. So why did I wish so much to take all of that away from Clem?

Chapter Two

THERE ARE many amazing things in this world, and we are one of them, but there are more. Some things that people don't know or don't believe in happen every day. Now, I could sit here all day, driving myself near mad, trying to make sense of it all, but there is no sense to be made.

There are legends of great magic and myths of adventures into other worlds. Why are they so hard to believe in?

"Now, Clem, I will leave California if I must. I will find somebody who will love me."

"Adam, you know I love you!"

"No, Clem—you're afraid of me."

He sighed. "You come here to my apartment to torment me?"

"No. Just to say one final farewell. Addio, Clem." I turned away.

"Adam!"

I turned to him and touched his shoulder. "Farewell."

"Adam, I don't want you to leave."

"One last time, Clem—farewell."

He sighed and turned away. I hoped I hadn't made him cry.

"Adam!" he yelled, running to the door. "How dare you walk away from me when I have something to say to you!"

"What do you have to say, Clem?"

"I have a lot to say," he answered. "Please don't leave."

"Clem, I must leave here. Everything I have grown to know is changing. I must find something more before I perish. The rising sun is beginning to look quite friendly to my immortal eyes."

"Don't do it, Adam!" he yelled. "You cannot!"

I turned away again.

"I *can't* take the blood, Adam. I'm sorry."

I nodded. He was crying his sweet mortal tears. The sight could have made me weep too, but I wouldn't allow it. I walked slowly back to Moonlight Manor and slept before dawn, not yet knowing where I planned to go.

Clem was brave; he would have made a beautiful vampire, a strong one. I wanted him as a companion, for how long would it be before Relone misses Verarsoe so much that he returns to him?

I waited for a time when I could explain this to Rayne and to Relone. I hoped for another chance to have my Clem—just one more chance to keep away from that word! I stopped by quite often, and each time I asked, he declined my offer. He said he wished to keep his human soul; he wanted the soul of a mortal, not a vampire. He spoke to me about God. He said he doesn't believe in him.

"Why is that, Clem?" I asked.

"Because—well because of you really."

"Me?"

"Yes."

"Don't let me take your faith from you, Clem. I want you to believe in God, whether I do or not. Whether it is important to me or not, I want it to be important to you."

"Why?" he asked, sounding offended.

"I meant no offense," I said. "I just want you to have peace, Clem, that's all—just peace. Please, Clem, tell me what I said to make you lose your faith."

"It was this," he said, handing me an old copy of my autobiography.

"You get rid of this!" I yelled. "Clement Hickman, I never want to see you reading this vile thing again!"

"It is not vile," he said. "It's fascinating. It's a beautiful memoir that opens my eyes to how cold the world can be, to how merciless life can be!"

"I don't want you reading it."

"Do you think that will stop me?"

I held it against my chest. "It will if you don't have it."

He sighed and fell into the chair behind him. "What if I don't believe in God because I don't want to?"

"If you were to say that, I wouldn't believe you," I answered.

He sighed again. "Maybe I don't want to."

"You may not want to," I started, "and if that be the case, you are telling yourself you don't believe in God simply because you don't want to, when in reality you believe in him more strongly than you feel you should!"

"And how do you know this, Mr. Arrogance?" He chuckled.

I smiled. "I don't. Just a theory."

He laughed. "You really are something, Adam Gold," he whispered, smiling. "You are something."

"Look at this beauty," I joked. "What can I say?"

He laughed loudly. "Come now, Adam. Tell me why —if you truly want me to believe in God—you want me to be like you."

"If you are made like me, I couldn't care less what you believe in," I said. "But as long as you are going to remain a fragile mortal, I want you to have God to turn to when there is nobody else."

"Maybe I do believe in God," he said quietly. "He is all I will have after you leave me."

"Your sisters?"

"I don't know," he said. "They don't give me much hope for Heaven."

"You need them, Clem, and don't be ridiculous. I'm not going to leave you."

"But you said—"

"Of course I said." I laughed. "It doesn't mean anything—you know that."

"Yes." He chuckled. "I guess I do."

"You know I love you too much to leave you."

"How much does *that* mean, Adam?"

"That actually means a lot. You know that."

"Yes—I guess I know that too."

I smiled. "You know, Clem, you know Relone came to see me in that chapel?"

"I did," he said with a laugh.

"I still sometimes ask myself why I did the things I did, why I still do the things I do."

"You are not the only one. I ask myself the same things. You see—some human."

"You ask yourself things, do you?"

"I do."

"But do you have ghastly answers, Clem?"

"Um…I…no. I guess I don't."

I sighed. "As I thought."

I wanted to tell Clement things—things I feared he would not understand.

"What sort of things?"

"Stop reading my thoughts." I laughed. "You don't need to know."

"That is why I want to."

"I can't tell you, Clem. You are mortal, and you are naïve."

"Naïve?"

"You are young and mortal, Clement. I do not need to burden you with things that worry me."

"You're worried?"

"What's the point in me denying it. You would know anyway. Really, Clem, I'm all right. I don't need to burden you with things right now or…ever for that matter."

"All right then. Never mind it."

When I awoke the next evening, I was delighted to see I was not alone. Clem sat right beside me, and as soon as I saw him, he was smiling.

"You speak Italian." He laughed.

"I'm from Switzerland," I answered, laughing back. "Of course I speak Italian."

"Addio?"

"It means farewell." I laughed a sleepy laugh and leaned in to embrace him.

"Yes, I know. I just wanted to tell you there is no need for a farewell now."

"And why is that, Clem?"

"You made me realize, Adam. I was up all night re-reading your story, and I see now that I can have both. I can make the best of my mortal years, and when there is no more, when there is nothing left, that does not mean I have to die—ever."

"Are you sure this is what you want, Clement?"

"I am sure."

I couldn't help but worry. Something wasn't right. Something felt very wrong.

"Tell me again, Clem…that you are sure."

"I am sure." He chuckled. "Now that I am sure, it is you who is not?"

I smiled, and a nervous excited feeling grew in the pit of my stomach. "I am sure that I want you. I just don't want you to make a mistake. Not that I believe this to be one, of course."

"I am sure. This will be no mistake."

"You will be strong, Clem. The power from Sekhmet and Lacara—it will take a lot of your lingering humanity before you have the chance to hold on to it. Hold on to as much as you can."

"You truly are the dark hero you think you are." He laughed.

"No," I answered. "I am Adam Gold, simply Adam Gold. I am powerful—but I am no hero!"

He just smiled. He was very charming when he looked at me that way.

"I have to admit to you, Adam—I am afraid, a little afraid."

"There is no need to fear," I said. "You will not die. Don't fight the changes, Clem, and there will be no pain!"

He shuddered. I planned to be gentle.

I smiled. "So tender," I whispered. I leaned in toward him and felt him shudder again. "So fragile and tender—so beautiful."

I was so close now that I could taste the salt and the metal. I could feel the blood pumping through his body. I felt the need to take his life, to end it and bring it into my own, but he drew away before I had time to.

"Be careful, Adam," he whispered, trembling. "Remember—I don't want to die."

"Just enough. Just enough to save you."

I leaned in again. I wanted the blood so badly now it was driving me near mad. Closer I came. I could smell it now—taste it. My hot breath upon his sweet mortal flesh, my teeth against his neck, I sank my teeth. Yes, made by me.

Chapter Three

HE LAY IN PAIN. There was this terrible thirst I knew he was feeling now, and he began to scream.

"Don't weep," I said to him kindly. I bit my wrist and placed it to his lips. "Just enough, Clem. Just enough."

He drank furiously; I could feel his pleasure as the blood rolled through his body, sweet as honey, thick, and hot. He felt warm now, warm and sleepy.

When I pulled away, I was sorry for the white shot of agony that came back to him. Every limb of his body convulsed until I thought he would be sick. He screamed and squirmed.

"It is only your mortal functions leaving your body," I whispered. "Don't worry. Remember what I said. Don't fight the changes."

The drum of his heartbeat pounded in my head, in unison with my own. But there was still pain—so much pain.

"Shh..." I soothed. "Look at me. Pay no attention to the pain. I know you are afraid, so very afraid, but this needs to happen. Don't be afraid anymore, Clem. Look at me—you are my child now, sweet Clem. Now you will look even more like my brother."

He tried to smile and reach out to me. I lifted him in my arms, as I knew he wanted me to, and cradled him until the pain was gone. He collapsed, nestled in the arms of his immortal brother.

Curse my immortal self.

I heard the intangible murmurs; he was mumbling nonsense. He said something about this being wonderful yet ghastly, something about how he was afraid.

"Clem—look." I smiled and handed him a hand mirror, the same as Victor had done for me so long ago.

He gasped but smiled as he ran his trembling fingers across his face and pierced his tongue with his fangs. Yes —perfectly sharp. He looked in fascination, and I was relieved to see he had not looked in horror as I had done two centuries ago.

I probably should have gone to see Relone that night, but I didn't, and I wished I had. Eric, an elder who I had met a few years before, had sent me a telegram from London, or rather he hadn't personally, but the return address was his.

Adam,

We need you here. No hatred between us. We call to you for urgent reasons. No questions asked.

~Verarsoe

. . .

Verarsoe was in London? As soon as I realized I was needed, a panicked feeling swept over me. *What had I done now?* Of course I was innocent; nothing wrong had been done by me. This was the truth, right? I didn't want to go to London, and I delayed, put it off until another telegram was sent to me.

Adam, where are you? This is urgent. Come immediately.
   ~Lacara

Lacara was with them. This really must have been serious. No more delaying. I knew they needed me, but for what? I sighed at these thoughts. *Eric, Verarsoe, and Lacara, what is going on?* Of course, I did delay even though I knew I shouldn't have. I delayed until I grew into fear that the elders would learn of my carelessness. I gathered my courage, and after letting Clem know I would be leaving, I asked that he not come with me.

"Adam, you don't mean that!" he said as I turned away

"Oh, yes, Clem," I answered. "If something has happened, I don't want you involved."

"I think you do. I think you want me to come with you."

"I don't, Clem."

"But you can't mean to leave me here on my own!"

"You'll be all right. You know what to do."

"No, Adam," he argued. "I want to come."

"No, Clem," I yelled. "I will say no more. I am leaving alone. Addio."

I embraced him. I silently left Clem's side.

I arrived in London near dawn; I was given the address of Eric's home. I was awakened very late in the night, and already another telegram had been sent to my hotel room. It had the address and house description written out for me once more. We would meet at the townhouse in Trafalgar Square. They had told me to be quick. I was nervous and could feel my heart pumping the blood to my cheeks, and I savored that human feeling even though it had badly irritated me. I knew I should be on my way back to California rather soon. I was afraid Clem might need me. He had access to Moonlight Manor and my townhouse in Salem too. He had the number of my agent and anything else he may need. I made sure he was in good hands, but still—I worried.

I dressed myself in the traditional baggy blue jeans and a white cotton T-shirt. I put a pair of dark sunglasses on, and taking the telegram with me, I left the hotel. It took me about an hour, walking slowly until I came to a small house with blue shutters and white stucco. I didn't like it much; it looked modern and synthetic. The moonlight danced upon the dirty shingles of the roof, and I almost wished I could have looked upon the night in London with mortal sight. I tried to keep my mind on the reason I had come. Before I even approached the door, a very familiar voice called my name. I turned that way.

"Adam!" he called, signaling me with his hand to

come inside. I obeyed immediately. "What took you so long?" he demanded.

"I walked slowly," I answered.

"This is no time for sarcasm!"

"Sorry. I really did walk slowly."

"Too slowly," I heard Eric say.

I just looked at him then back at Relone.

"I'm here now," I said.

"You are," Relone answered. "But where is Rayne?"

"She's in Salem," I said. "She said something about gathering some things from our townhouse. She'll be back."

I noticed everybody was there—Victor, Relone, Lacara, and now me. There was also one I had not met before, but I could see the love between him and Victor. He must have been who Victor talked about in his journal. I had never seen Victor this way before. He was smiling; he was happy. He touched the hand of who I thought to be Daniel and smiled. I laughed inside myself when I saw a tiny child crawl up on Victor's lap and hand him a trinket. My maker embraced the child and wiped the tears from his eyes. What was going on? Victor had a child? After placing the trinket in his shirt pocket, he handed the lovely child a yellow hair ribbon. I shook off the confusion and pulled my gaze from Victor back to Eric.

"What on earth was so damned important that you should call me from California?"

"Adam, please," Relone started. Lord how I had missed him. "Let us begin."

"I wasn't disagreeing," I said. "I was just asking what—"

He put his hand up to silence me and nodded, telling

me *all right.* I looked at Eric—small in build, black wavy hair, and almost piercing green eyes staring at me from across the way. Those eyes almost seemed to have layers to them, and if I were to push through to the last layer, I would find anger or fear or something somewhere in them, but I couldn't. He remained rock solid and completely strong and unafraid. It clashed with the fear in the eyes of the beautiful Lacara and even the discomfort in Relone's, the uneasiness in Verarsoe's, and the confusion in my own. Something had happened, but nobody would speak yet. Nobody knew where to start.

As we sat at that little round table, all eyes were on me. Not even Relone looked warm toward me.

"Please," I started. "Will somebody tell me what the hell is going on here!" I wanted to stand to my feet, to yell. "This bloody meeting has been pointless thus far."

"Mon dieu," Relone whispered. "What have you done now?"

I stared at Verarsoe, my old friend and enemy, and Daniel, the stranger in Victor's diary, and the lovely immortal child who I guessed to be Anna. She also had a diary I had found. Then there was my beloved Relone, made by Verarsoe, and Eric, the very modern elder. It was hard for me to believe this very creature had walked the streets of Troy so many centuries ago.

"I have done nothing wrong!" I yelled. "I have told no secrets nor broken any rules."

"That's your first mistake," said Eric. "First of all, you speak to mortals. You tell them our secrets."

"My stories earn the 'Fiction' title, Eric."

He sighed. "Something has happened!"

"Well, then tell me already," I snapped. "Nothing has been made of this meeting so far, and Clem may need me." I said it before I could stop myself.

"Clem?" I heard Relone yell. "Clement Hickman?"

I only sighed.

"Adam, I'm not so sure you should have done that," Eric started.

No response. What *had* I done this time?

"Ali and Maggie Hickman," he continued. "I'm assuming you know them."

"Yes."

"They're witches."

"And?"

"And this Clem of yours…?"

"No," I answered. "He is just a gifted boy, now a strong vampire made by me."

"That's why we called you here," said Verarsoe. "We wanted to prevent this."

"Why?" I yelled. "What the hell did I do wrong this time?"

"It's not that it was wrong," Relone retorted with a raise of the eyebrows. "It's just that it shouldn't have been done just yet. Now Clem is going to be involved in the most terrible event our kind has ever seen!"

"What?"

"You know Sekhmet may strike. We didn't want to risk it."

"So you called me to London?"

"Yes," Eric answered. His eyes flashed, and it frightened me for a moment. I suddenly felt his age as I hadn't before, and it passed through me coldly, forcing a harsh breath from my lips.

"We called you here because…" He sighed and held out his hand. "May I see it, Adam—the medallion, I mean."

An odd sense of anger washed over me. I felt invaded and offended. I wanted to strike out at him, to beat him to where he couldn't move, but that feeling left so soon I began to wonder if it had ever really been there at all.

"Are you all right?" Relone asked. I heard the concern in his voice.

"Yes," I answered, shaking off the sensations. "Yes… I'm fine."

"So may I see it?" Eric asked again, extending his hand farther toward me and raising his thick, dark eyebrows at me. His eyes stared at me with that unfathomable age. What did he want with my sacred medallion?

I took the medallion off my neck and held it tightly in my hand. I held it out to him, but it was as if my fingers wouldn't allow me to let it go. The metal burned into the palm of my hand, and I wanted to keep it close to me; it was a part of me now. I closed my eyes and held out my hand, still squeezing it with all my strength. Eric took it from my grasp with ease, and I gasped, not realizing he didn't even notice my strength. I wanted it back; I began to feel a nervous kind of pain. It did nothing for him even as he closed his eyes and held it against his chest. He ran his fingers softly over the engraving, frustrated it didn't do what he expected. As soon as he gave it back, I felt that strength and comfort cascade over me.

"It is time, Adam," Eric started. "And you need not ask what I mean."

"I realize that," I answered. "But please tell me—what *have* I done?"

Relone sighed, and the others looked to him as if asking how to respond.

"You did nothing wrong, my love," he said. "But you must understand, Adam, there is something you must do now. You must break away, become the leader of this era, become who you were born to be, by Victor Miller himself. You were made to lead these times, to lead us into a time of peace."

Eric looked frightened now; his eyes showed true fear, and it made my beautiful eyes weld with tears. Instantly, he became solid and emotionless again, and it frightened me. I couldn't help but wonder now what they would ask of me, what they were about to tell me. Everybody stared at one another as if not a single thought could pass from their lips that would make any sense. Every single elder was frightened, and Victor's child stared at me the way Madeline used to stare at me—with compassion, confusion, and sorrow. She was but a vampire child, capable of so much more than could possibly be known, and she sent me images through her mind of Victor's castle and the old teddy bear on the tattered mattress. She was telling me who she was. Yes, Anna. She was Victor's sweet, beloved Anna.

I looked to Victor, and he averted his eyes. I looked to Relone, and his face became sad. I looked to Lacara, and she shook her head before dropping her gaze to the floor. I looked to Eric; he stared at me until I moved my gaze away. I didn't know what to say or what to think. All I knew was another age of the dark world was about to begin, and how I was to handle this I had no idea. And mon dieu my poor Clem. Why did I have to bring him to me at such a vile and perilous time? Relone took a breath as he prepared to speak. I tried to read his thoughts, but it was hopeless.

The battle was coming, I told myself. My blood ran cold; the time was right before me, waiting for me.

There was much wrong in what I had done to Clem and so much wrong in all that was going to happen. But I asked myself continuously—whose fault was this? Who was to blame for the horror of the century, the terror that she would rain upon us? It could not possibly be me —could it?

My mind flashed with pictures of Clem, and I looked to my master, begging him to tell me now what he wanted so badly to tell me. My eyes were tear filled, and my expression was painfully sad.

Relone stared at me. "The time has come, Adam," he said. "Now is the hour in which all Hell is before you, awaiting a battle. Now she comes. Prepare for The Mother herself."

"Oh, my beloved Clem," I wept. "What have I done to you?"

Chapter Four

I CAN'T TELL you when first I awoke, when exactly I came to, realizing I was not at home. I awoke knowing she and I had been together in ways that would cause pain to my black-haired love back home if ever she were to learn of it.

She smiled a beautiful, fanged smile, and it made me shudder and gasp. I knew I had been crying, but I couldn't remember why. She held me in her arms and took me North—or I thought it was North. When she lowered me to the ground, I realized I was in a stone room—like a dungeon.

"Where...?"

"Don't ask," she answered. "It matters not. What is important is that we are together now, and I can tell you what I want. You have a power, Adam Gold, a power I adore, and with you as my king, ruling beside me, we can have the power to rule the dark world. We have the power to create our own world, so the only undead beauties will be our children."

"You mean...start over?" I asked. "Re-make the undead?"

"Yes," she answered. "Re-make the dark world and destroy all not made by us and all who oppose us. I will spare only those you love. You will rule the world now, Adam Gold—the world!"

"A che cosa mi serve?" I mumbled under my breath.

"What is that to you?" she yelled.

I hadn't realized she understood Italian.

"I know you desire power, Adam. I know you do! Don't you see? We can create a new world—but first we must destroy the old."

"Why?"

"For all to bow to us," she said. "Destroy all who are not our children, for if all are made by us, then all will be bound to us, and at last I can have that long-desired power, my king, that power I deserved so many eons ago. It was my fate to have it—my destiny!"

"I don't believe it," I said.

"And why not?" she asked, her glowing, amber eyes making me tremble.

"We cannot destroy our own kind. It is the vilest of crimes. They cannot all follow you, Sekhmet. They will rise above us. There is just too much wrong with it. It *can't* work."

"Of course it will work, my dark king. Why do you fear so much?"

I wasn't afraid; I was confused. She had snatched me up again and taken me with her to help her fulfill her devious plans, but I couldn't leave her. She had a sort of power over me; her beauty captivated me, and I couldn't leave her.

"I need you to obey me, Adam," she said. "And if you do, you will understand why it isn't possible for them to refuse me. Now, do not speak. I have something I must ask you."

A dark chill came over me, passing through me painfully. I tried to distract myself from the fact that she looked like a walking chunk of sculpted marble, and I listened again.

"Your old strengths are not needed," she said. "Not with this new power you have possessed over the centuries you have lived. Believe in yourself, Adam. You don't realize how much power you truly have!"

I dropped my gaze. I couldn't look at her. The evil in her eyes frightened me, and I didn't know what to say in response to her words, if they had even been words at all.

"Do you remember when you wanted to do good far and wide? When you wanted to have people look upon you as a god?"

"Yes, I remember."

"Well, now you can have that love, Adam. You can have our beautiful kind look upon you as their god, their creator—their *one true master*!"

For some reason, there was no room for me to argue or protest at all. I couldn't understand why I couldn't respond. I was frightened now, weeping, clinging to her, begging her not to make me do this. I was terrified now of what she would ask of me.

I knew we were in a church. I didn't know how I knew, but I knew. I didn't know where or why, and her beauty and grace continued to draw me into her arms whenever I became cold toward her.

"Look at that broken piece of glass there," she said in

her ringing voice. It almost hurt my ears to listen, and I enjoyed that feeling. Upon the dusty, crumbling floor of the church was a piece of red glass from the broken window beside me. I could see it had once been a portrait of Christ with his arms reaching toward the sky, with a beautiful angel on each side of him. I wanted to look at the window not the glass, but I obeyed.

"Yes…?"

"Now, tell yourself you want that glass," she said, "that you want that glass more than anything."

"What?"

"Trust me. Do as I say."

I stared at that worthless piece of glass on the floor. I didn't want it, but I had to obey. I imagined the glass was the Christ floating above the ground, with his arms reaching toward the sky. Nothing happened, but I kept my focus, not able to pry my eyes away. A trembling resonance echoed through the church, and I felt as if the building was about to collapse. I felt like that gorgeous window would fall to pieces over my head, but I couldn't take my eyes off that glass.

"Adam," I heard her whisper.

I ignored.

"Stop," she said, her voice swelling. "Adam—stop!"

That feeling that the building would fall apart came back to me, and the floorboards were shaking fiercely, but I couldn't stop now. I saw that piece of glass from the window beside me and found myself screaming and throwing my arms in front of my face. The crashing of shattered glass assaulted my ears, and shards pricked my skin. I slowly lowered my arms to see the beautiful window really had fallen to pieces over my head.

Sekhmet would be angry. I couldn't look at her. I was terrified of her wrath.

"You didn't do as I said," she whispered, but she was calm.

I brought my gaze back into her eyes, and instantly a chill passed through me. I had forgotten how beautiful she was in the few moments I had been staring at the floor.

"I'm sorry," I whispered, bowing my head. "I couldn't want the glass."

"What do you want, my love?"

"The window," I said. "I want the window with Christ and his angels."

"Do you now?" She laughed, and it hurt my ears.

I nodded.

"Then let yourself have it," she whispered.

I stared at the shattered glass and imagined what I wanted. I began to shake, and the blood sweat broke out all over my body when I saw the glass…was moving—first in random circular and zigzag like motions. But as the seconds passed, the pieces were fitting into each other like a puzzle, and slowly the crumbling dusty floor at my feet became a beautiful portrait of the Christ with his golden-haired angels. I smiled, trying to recall the way I had done this thing in front of me, trying to understand how any of this was possible—by me, Adam Gold.

"My sweet Lord!" I whispered. "How…?"

Sekhmet was smiling now. I couldn't stop staring at the window. That once worthless piece of red stained glass had now become the flowing sleeve of the dress—the dress that Christ's angel was wearing. I was puzzled by the thought of how something so worthless could become so valuable in a matter of seconds. And I loved that piece of glass now, but I didn't tell it to come to me. I told it to stay right there as the angel's pretty, flowing dress.

The Mother hadn't spoken yet, and I didn't know what else she wanted me to do, but I was distracted by these thoughts when my sight captured a different image. Another window, one across the way, was also a portrait of the Christ, only this one…made me sad; it made me furious! It was that man upon the cross with anguish and pain in his sweet, dead face. I told it what I wanted, that I wanted it to break. And slowly, small spider webs of cracks spread across the picture, and I told it to shatter. The floor below us was now covered with those glimmering pieces of glass, instantly in a more beautiful and random design that meant nothing to anyone yet meant so much to me—because *I* had made it!

"You see?" she said at last. "You can extend your powers to measures you never thought possible and would never had been able to learn of without me."

I was trembling now, but it was in excitement, and I was suddenly feeling very warm toward her, and I brought myself into her arms, this time without her help.

I was afraid now—afraid of her strength, of her power. It was maddening. Something must be done. I am Adam Gold. I can resist anything—can't I? I have never surrendered to anybody—have I? But the more I was with her, the more I began to like—and even crave—the idea of power.

36

"You do want it, don't you, Adam?" she whispered. I knew what she meant.

"No," I said. "I don't want to destroy!" I was lying. I did want this. I wanted to have beauty such as this love me for my strength and my power, but this was wrong—wasn't it? She had a power over me, a power that took me away from all reason and led me astray onto a path of wild passion and desire. All I knew was what I wanted, what I craved. I knew what would happen; it was as I always feared. Our secrets would be scattered across the globe, and our race would be destroyed, if not by each other, then by hunters we could not escape.

"You underestimate my power, Adam," she said. "You don't see my strength, do you?"

"Actually, it is quite the contrary," I stated. "There is no use in me denying it. You will read it in my mind anyway. It is because I know you will do this well, and I'm afraid that you may succeed. And that frightens me more than you failing. It truly horrifies me."

"There is no need for fear now, my night prince. We cannot begin this way, not here. I will take you to another part of the world, and we will begin there."

Instantly, I began to cry again. I clutched her shoulder to keep from falling over. She embraced me and cradled my head against her chest.

"Remember, Adam," she whispered in my ear. "Believe!"

Chapter Five

SHE KISSED AWAY MY TEARS, tasting my blood for her own delight. I wasn't frightened anymore, but I was lost, and her beauty confused me. The ruby jewel about her neck hung low, lying gently upon her lower chest, where her white gown clung to her like part of her body. I stared at her beautifully shaped arms with the golden snakes coiled delicately around them. Her black hair hung loosely over her shoulders and down her back.

"Who are you?" she asked, drawing me into her arms.

"I don't know," I answered. "I am Adam Gold. Nothing more."

"You were chosen to lead this era. Did you know that, Adam Gold?"

I didn't respond.

"If not by Victor Miller, then by somebody else. We have been waiting for somebody like you. You were chosen to lead us into this new age. I can see you. Can you see yourself?"

"No," I answered, looking away again. "I cannot."

She smiled, drawing me to her eyes again, deep shimmering, golden eyes. She moved the long, black strands of hair behind my ears and smoothed them above my forehead so she could stare into my eyes.

"You shouldn't hide such beautiful eyes behind your hair that way."

"Where are we?" I asked.

"That doesn't matter," she said. "But our kind dwell here, and they will be put to fire now."

I sighed. "Please," I pleaded, desperation dripping from my words. "I beg of you. Do not make me do this. I don't want to hurt anyone, Sekhmet."

And once again I was wrapped in her arms, feeling my will depleting. I was warm and comfortable. I didn't feel lost in her arms; I felt as if I knew exactly where I was. I didn't want her to let go. I clung to her like a child.

She pushed me away and spoke to me softly.

"We are far from California now, my Adam," she said. "Look to the crumbling stone of the walls. Look to the ancient bricked road."

"Where on Earth are we?" I demanded.

"You know where we are," she answered. "Your body, your soul, knows this land."

I stumbled and clung to the crumbling wall beside me, watching the pebbles and crumbs fall at my feet. Her desire for power, her obsession for overpowering Ké Hé Zule, that's what this was all about. She wanted to show all that she was more powerful than The Father, and this is where she began.

It was icy cold out, and the sky was filled with clouds my gifted eyes could easily see—gray clouds. I was expecting rain.

"Come," she whispered. "Find the immortals. Show your true power. I know your hidden lust for power. Tell me now, Adam—don't you want it?"

I didn't answer her, couldn't answer her. I wouldn't do this. Not me. I would never do what she asked. She took me above the city, high into the clouds, and pointed out to me actual coven houses where our kind dwelled— underground mansions, secret catacombs, and innocent clubs nobody suspected were filled with blood hunters.

"Set fire to their flesh," she whispered.

I saw the flames in her eyes, and it filled me with more terror than I could possibly express. And below us, flames spread through the city, and the cries of the creatures rang in my mind, and I cried and cried. I clung to The Mother and begged her to stop. When I saw her eyes were gentle again, I stared at her, waiting for what I knew she was going to say.

"You do it," she said. "You do it."

"No," I whispered, still crying. "I can't. I won't."

"Do it, Adam," she said again. "Show your strength. Are you the Adam Gold I think you are? Or are you just a coward?"

How could she do this to me? Mocking me so I would obey? I knew I wasn't a coward; she knew it too. I refused to let this work on me. I would not surrender simply to prove to her my power and strength that she already knew I possessed.

I strengthened my grip on her dress. "Please." I tried to resist. I tried to turn away from her. I tried with every ounce of strength I possessed but to no avail. There was nothing within me stronger than her will. I squeezed my eyes shut, pain and guilt overflowing inside me.

I used my power to collapse roofs and walls of the burning buildings into the now escaping vampires.

"Don't you dare close your eyes," she whispered kindly. "Never close eyes so beautiful."

I tried to obey, but it was as if my eyes were glued shut. I kept trying with no success. My body burned with fear of what Sekhmet would do for not minding her.

"Open your eyes!" she repeated, shouting this time.

My eyelids slowly lifted as if by some outside source, and I was forced to look upon what I had done.

All those magnificent, terrible creatures screaming and fleeing. Pain tore at my chest, but it was mingled with a terrible excitement—a thirst for more. It was pure power, pure will. Anything I wanted, I could take for myself.

My hands shook from the excitement. There was almost grief, almost a need to mourn, but I had gone too far now. I burned them, collapsed buildings on them, tormented them, frightened them.

I saw it—an immortal of gray hair; he was an old man when he was turned. I watched him dodging debris, his eyes wide with fear and confusion. He tripped over his own feet as he tried to move through the rubble. I spotted a cracked window in a building behind him. I calmly told it to break and sent a large shard flying toward the immortal, immediately severing his head, letting it topple and roll amongst the ruins of the city. Blood pooled around his now lifeless body, flowing down the streets.

Mortals screamed and fainted. I didn't hurt them though. I had no concern for the humans. I was to destroy those who were not bound to us—my queen and me.

All in one night, I destroyed immortals by the

hundreds. I felt stained with their blood, drenched in their filth. But I was clean. I glanced at my hands and my shirt. Perfectly clean. The feeling of evil coursed through me, and for the first time—it felt good.

It lasted only until I looked to Sekhmet to see she was smiling, and it tortured me—tortured me so deeply I began to cry. What was I becoming?

As Sekhmet watched the fires burn through the city and listen to the sirens rolling down the streets, she seemed to not even notice me, so I clung to her, wrapped my arms around her, and cried myself dry.

Chapter Six

SHE LOOKED at me and told me I was under her command now. She fed me her blood, and although I hadn't needed the blood of mortals in a very long time, her power was sustaining me, and I loved the fact I was not hungry.

I tried to look back on how this had happened, on how all of this was heaped upon me so quickly without any warning. I had been weeping for days without stopping, weeping and clinging to her. She laughed at me, and I hated it because I didn't know what it meant. How could beauty such as this love who I am? Actually love the literal evil that I am? Oh, it made me feel incredible yet wildly confused me at the same time. Now, do not think I don't know I am adored far and wide—oh no. I see the pretty little mortals sound asleep with my memoir sitting on a nightstand or neglected at the foot of the bed, with its place held by a colorful plastic bookmark. I see their faces as they read; I see their concern when I am in danger, their jealousy when I am in love, and their adoration when I am happy. I see the way they smile. And yes, of course I hear their calls. But now as I stood here in this room, I couldn't believe that beauty such as this wanted anything to do with me. She hadn't spoken of where we were yet; she hadn't spoken much at all. I stood out upon the balcony and stared down at the dark waters and green trees. We were on an island of some kind. I didn't know where. I realized by the mist from the sea and the smell of the air that we were somewhere off the coast of the Caribbean—in a hotel perhaps.

Silence and tears came again, but she didn't laugh at me this time. I didn't know why I was crying. I tried to ask her where we were, but she didn't respond. I didn't want to kill that night. I didn't want to be the one to lead this era; I wanted to be the one who slept in a bed, unaware of the evil the world was facing.

Relone had told me to break away, hadn't he? He had told me to lead our kind into an age of peace, but that was not possible.

As the days passed on, I still felt as if I were inside a dream. I awoke every evening feeling tired, and my eyes were always wet with tears. Nothing made sense; it was like I was living life through the eyes and mind of a madman.

I dreamed a lot while I slept; I heard the voices of my family. I had been dreaming about blood as I usually did. I had been dreaming of destroying. I had killing on my mind. I had power in my heart.

"What's it saying, my king?" she asked me, awaking me slowly.

"It is saying to stop this, to go home," I answered. "It is saying that I am not meant for this task, my love."

She chuckled. "Oh no you don't," she answered. "This is your task. If that's what these dreams are saying, then do not listen to them. Listen to me, Adam Gold. You are under my command now, and there is nothing that will change that. As I have said, you were chosen to lead this era, and I am the partner of Ké Hé Zule himself. Therefore, I as well was chosen to rule, and so together we will take our world into our hands, and all will obey and bow to us and us alone. We are the owners of the night now, my love, only you and I. There are no others amongst us who share our power."

"And why do you say this?" I asked. "Why do you say I was chosen to rule?"

"Because you were," she answered. "Because you were meant to be here. You were meant to be made. If it hadn't been Victor, it would have been Relone. Don't be ridiculous, Adam. You already know this."

I sighed. "I do. Perhaps I just don't want to believe it."

"And why is that? Tell me—don't you agree that ruling our world after recreating it will put an end to the terror and misery of the undead?"

"No. They don't need a god."

"Yes, they do. They need a ruler. Wouldn't it, though, Adam, put an end to the terror and the pain of the undead?"

"There will always be creatures in pain," I said. "No matter who their ruler is, there will always be those who hate what they are, who fear themselves more than you."

"Not if we choose wisely."

I sighed. "No, Sekhmet. You are not right—not this time."

"And why must you be so difficult?" she yelled. "You are the true definition of a vampire. You know it."

"I am not!" I yelled. "You want the true definition of a vampire, take me home and snatch up Verarsoe."

She laughed again. "No, Adam. You do not understand how strong you really are."

I sighed again and turned away. "I don't care to know."

Chapter Seven

I KNEW I had been feeding off her like a hungry, wild animal, and she held me in her arms as if I were hers for the taking and hers alone. And all the while, there were no thoughts of Rayne even crossing my mind or skipping by in my memory.

We were headed westward now, but that didn't matter. Nothing mattered when I was in her arms. It was like being inside a dream, where nothing makes sense, but you still don't want to wake up.

Her blood was the most powerful of all, and through it, she had given me strength—strength to do unspeakable things. The faces of those I destroyed haunted me.

News of this overflowed the television and radio stations. It was all talk of mysterious fires that spread through the cities and people who have claimed to have heard the victims screaming, "Curse thee! Curse thy demon of Satan! Curse thy queen!"

Of course, Sekhmet found all of this very funny and laughed almost as though she couldn't stop.

"You see?" she started. "They do fear me, and soon, they will fear you too."

"Fear me?"

"And then you can have that new love, when all but our children are destroyed—save the precious few you love."

"Our secrets, my queen," I whispered.

"Yes?"

"Our secrets—they will be scattered across the globe. They will be released into a world of light and thrown upon an unsuspecting world. This plan will throw open the doors of darkness and release all we have paid in blood to keep hidden from the mortal world."

"Do not fear so much, Adam," she whispered, kissing my cheek. "It will be all right."

"It can't be," I said. "Please don't let me do this. There is too much wrong with this. I do not want to be evil."

"But evil is what we are," she said. "It is what we have always been. Do you believe you deserve to die?"

"I do."

"And yet you do nothing. You think you deserve to die, but you let yourself live. You let yourself thrive on the blood of the innocent. That, Adam Gold…does that make you evil?"

"It does."

"Then I have made myself clear."

There was a tingling nervous worry inside of me, but I tried to push it aside, to ignore it until it went away. Night after night, I destroyed vampires by the hundreds, and night after night, I wept the smile off both our faces.

I knew Sekhmet was evil. I kept telling myself I could

choose to not be. I kept telling myself I could make my own choices and turn her away when I wished it. I soon learned it was not possible. I was shackled to her. She had an unnatural hold on me that I could not escape. I could not explain how I fell weak around her. I asked myself over and over why I couldn't be the one in control.

"Because you are young," she answered in response to my thoughts.

"Damn! Would you not do that?" I yelled. I was soon afterward a bit embarrassed by this reaction. I hadn't even realized she was standing there, let alone reading my thoughts.

"Come now," she started. "It is time once again."

She took me above the city, and as I peered down at the lights below, I thought of all the vampires who existed on Earth. Less than half I knew, and half of those I loved.

I had a chance for so many friendships, companions, and so many chances for those to teach me other ways of existing. Other ways to cope with eternity. And now— now I was destroying all of that.

Sekhmet had taken me through the streets of the city and showed me the evil, the poverty, as well as the love and relief. She showed me the homeless and the rich. She showed me everything.

I killed over and over that night, destroying thousands of immortals, and Sekhmet's beauty was growing as her improvement increased. I stared at all those beautiful creatures as I burned and broke their bodies. As I waited for my queen's next commandment, I felt a smile force its way onto my face, but I let it.

I gazed at my hands and looked back to that long-ago night on the ship when Victor had first made me. I remembered only finding comfort in my blue eyes, knowing that was the only thing that looked as it did when I was still alive. I saw my face in my mind, saw my blue eyes, and I couldn't believe that I, Adam Gold, had done this. But this time, there was hardly a trace of guilt. No longer did I feel a need to burn; no longer did I want to die. I was so confused, so terribly puzzled that I had changed so much so quickly. I wanted the old Adam back. I wanted to feel that guilt. It was the only human emotion I still possessed—compassion—but it was gone now.

Rage followed afterward; my confusion had caused madness. My anger caused me to burn all the harsher as I yelled and threw my hands toward the city, shattering glass as I screamed, drawing blood from my ears. But Sekhmet only smiled, and I could feel the flames within my eyes when I turned toward her, glaring at her with that scowl on my face, and once again I found myself closed within her arms.

She had taken me out again to show me the world. This time, she showed me the suffering. The city was nothing but poverty. I didn't know where we were. We moved on and came to a hospital.

"You must understand," she said. "People die, Adam. People suffer everyday so much worse than you do. They suffer, and they die. You must accept that."

"I do."

"Prove it," she said. "Step into a room and see what's lying in the bed."

I entered the hospital and let myself slip into the room unnoticed. In the bed lay a sleeping child—a boy with thick, dark hair. He was lovely; he had round little eyes that moved as he dreamed. I looked into his mind, and I found comfort. He was dreaming—of dying. And die he soon would, as he wished and prayed for night after night because he would never feel better. I couldn't take it. A beautiful, innocent child. His eyes were surrounded in dark gray circles. His lips were black. His bones shone through his clothes. He was sick. I could barely stand to look at him this way. I didn't want to see him hurt. I didn't want to see him die.

I wanted to wake him up, but he was at peace as he slept. I crept a little closer, and he awoke under my touch. As soon as his brown eyes opened, there were tears.

"Shh," I whispered, stroking his hair. "Don't cry. What's your name?"

"Charlie." His voice was thin and fragile. The look in his eyes told me he knew I was different. He could see that white complexion of my skin and the glow in my eyes. He could see I did not look alive.

"Do you know what will happen after this, Charlie?"

"Will I hurt?"

"Never again."

"Don't let the doctors come back," he said as the tears began pouring from his beaming, innocent eyes. "Don't let them hurt me anymore. I just want to be left alone. I just want to go to Jesus now."

I knew my blood was powerful, but unfortunately, Charlie was too sick. My blood could not heal him. There was only one thing left for me to do.

"My name is Adam. I can give you that wish."

"Please, angel," he replied, forcing the words from his lips. "Tell my sister she doesn't have to wait for me anymore. Tell her I'm coming. Please, angel, when you go back to Heaven, will you take me with you?"

My heart broke, and tears filled my own eyes. This was so unfair. I knew I could not deny his request. I did not care what point Sekhmet was trying to make. She was wrong. I did not have to accept anything I could change.

I heard her voice in my head. *Don't do it, Adam.*

"Of course I will, Charlie," I whispered. "Close your eyes, and when you open them, you will be there."

I searched his mind once again, just to be sure he was ready. I leaned forward and pricked his neck. All of his pain flowed into me, suffocating me for a moment. I gasped for breath, gripping the bed to stabilize myself.

Charlie was now gone—at peace with his sister in that beautiful place I will never see. I knew Sekhmet would be angry, but I didn't care. I couldn't stop now. I had to do penance for the pain I had caused.

I found the other rooms in the same ward. All of these children were terminal. All of them deserved peace. I continued to ignore Sekhmet's protests and ventured down the corridor to the next child who needed an angel. It was not an easy task in the least, but it felt right.

I left the intensive care unit and headed toward another ward. I opened the door silently to see a lovely, young girl lying in the bed.

"Are you a doctor?" she asked coldly.

"I am. Are you hurting?"

She shook her head, her eyes tightening with tears. "I just don't want to die alone."

"Oh no, chére," I whispered, stroking her hair. "You're not going to die."

"Yes, I am," she answered with strength behind her words, ceasing her tears. "I'm not afraid. Everybody dies. I am only afraid of dying with nobody by my side."

"I am by your side."

She smiled. "I thank you for that, but please—can you bring me Ethan?"

"Ethan?"

"My brother. I asked before, but they said they couldn't reach him. If you can try again…"

"Say no more."

After calling her brother, I waited outside the room. I could still hear Sekhmet's warnings. I took a few deep breaths, trying to calm my nerves. God only knew what she would do to me for this.

When Ethan arrived, I listened in on what sounded like a reconciliation of sorts. It was heartwarming to see them reconnecting, but it broke my heart at the same time.

"Excuse me," I said, entering the room. "May I have a moment alone with the patient?"

Ethan furrowed his brow. "Can I come back?"

"In a moment." I leaned in toward her. "Are you in pain?"

"No, but…I think I lied before."

"About the pain?"

"No. About not being afraid to die. I don't want to die."

"I know," I whispered. "I told you, chére, you are not going to die."

She just stared at me. I could see her wide emerald

eyes were brimmed with unshed tears. I reached for a syringe on the cart beside the door. I inserted the needle into my arm, filling it with my blood.

"I'm going to give you something for the pain," I said.

"I told you. I'm not in any pain. Please, just bring Ethan back."

"I'm a doctor. Trust me."

I pressed the needle into the port for her IV, watching the liquid flow down into her bloodstream.

"I'll go get your brother. And no—you are not going to die."

I smiled at her and left the room. I nodded to Ethan, and within the smile he gave me, I felt he knew what I was telling him. His sister would live to see many more days of happiness.

I returned to Sekhmet, fearing her wrath. I knew what I had done was worth it. How could I change my fate if I did not do as much good as I was able? I looked down at my feet, too afraid to look into her eyes.

"You do not understand," she scolded.

The irritation in her voice was dark and powerful. I had forgotten the sound of her voice. My memory never did it justice. I trembled.

"You do not understand that people suffer and are meant to suffer."

"Why do you say this?" I pressed with too much defiance in my tone. "Nobody is meant to suffer. Nobody deserves to be in pain. That is, of course—except for us."

"I know you have this belief of there being good in all creatures. I see your obsession with goodness. I understand you believe all people deserve to feel joy, Adam, but it just isn't so."

"And who are you to decide that?"

An immediate mask of rage began taking shape, stripping away her beauty. It was no more than a fraction of a second, and it passed so quickly I wondered if I had imagined it. I cringed and felt the regret of my words. Questioning Sekhmet was the most unwise thing I could do.

"People die every day," she said. "Don't you believe if they were not meant to die, they wouldn't?"

"I don't. We are not meant to be here, Sekhmet. We are abominations cast out from God. Things that are not meant to happen, happen all the time."

"You want to change that?"

"I want to make my own choices. I want to help mortals. If that means I have to kill them to do so, then it is nothing I haven't done before."

She smiled, ripping away my strength. My knees buckled, but she held me up. "You love too much."

Chapter Eight

I AWOKE IN TEARS, or maybe I had been awake but came to myself when I realized I had been crying once more. She told me again I was meant to lead the new era. She told me if Victor hadn't found me, there would have been another who would. I didn't know who I was anymore. I wanted to do good far and wide, but I had loved the destruction I had caused. I loved the power, and I hated that I loved it.

"Sekhmet," I choked out...or I tried to. I was unsure if I had spoken at all or if I was even breathing. She didn't answer, so I called out to her again. I closed my eyes, and when I opened them again, I was in her arms. "No!" I tried to say. "Please—don't make me do this. I...I..."

"Shh," she soothed. "Sleep, my blue-eyed beauty."

No. Please listen to me. Oh please, my queen, my beautiful one, I wanted to say, but I couldn't. I was losing consciousness. I tried to force myself to stay awake. I could feel by my bones what time it was, and I realized dawn was not far.

I knew Sekhmet was a liar who wanted nothing but power, and suddenly a very familiar phrase came into my mind, a phrase that sounded even more beautiful the more times I recited it in my mind.

If ever life becomes unbearable—there is always the rising sun.

Twilight—the sky was still blue when I awoke, and it had rained during the day, for the streets were still wet. My only other alternative it seemed was to sell myself to the sunlight. Nothing good could come from me as long as I remained under control of The Mother. It was time.

Another night of killing took place, and as The Mother slept, or lay on the ground of the city, I decided it was as good a time as any to take my chance and destroy myself before my evil destroyed the world.

I crawled out of my sleeping place, all covered and caked with dirt. I took a few moments to brush the impossible stains from my clothes and stood there with my arms outstretched and my eyes closed. A great light flooded the sky. I opened my eyes; I could see the sun. For the first time in over two hundred years, I could see the sun.

A laugh erupted from my chest, followed by a practical fit of hysteria. The light seemed to engulf the entire earth. It blinded me, but it was beautiful—magnificent. With the beauty of this, there was more. There was pain. The rays dripped upon my skin like acid. I fell to my knees as the rays began puncturing my flesh like a million needles.

I had to endure it. I could not give up. I would let myself suffer as I deserved, and when my bones turned to ashes, all would be forgiven. My skin bubbled and bled. I screamed, but I loved the pain. I thought of the church I had destroyed. I thought of Jesus with his angels in the beautiful red dresses.

I deserved this. It felt as if I were being cleansed, purified, purged of all the wrong I had done.

I would endure this agony until my bones turned to ashes and those ashes were swept into the sea.

I yelled out, "Bring me pain!"

I remembered the beautiful Katie Hunter with her beaming brown eyes whom I had murdered in New York City the night I had gone to find Maggie. Yes—bring me pain!

My flesh felt as if it was slowly melting away and sliding off my bones layer by layer, and I waited for Mary, waited to see her one last time before the doors of Hell opened before me, but she did not come.

Every nerve in my body craved blood. The world fell away, and all that remained was the insatiable thirst, the unrelenting need to heal my broken body.

Blood, blood, and blood.

"I'm here now, my love." I heard the voice clear as a bell though my mind was still foggy.

"Mary," I forced from my chest. My lungs were so

scorched almost no sound escaped. "Mary, my love. Forgive me."

"Shh," I heard her soothe. "Lie still, Adam. Lie quiet. You are wounded. Open your eyes."

"What?"

"Open your eyes!"

I opened my eyes and groaned when I saw Sekhmet's stunning face. I turned away.

"I suppose you think that was terribly clever of you!"

"Please," I said. "You should have let me die!"

"Do you think that would have killed you?"

"Of course I do!"

She sighed. "Well, now just look at what you have done. You've really upset our plans."

"*Your* plans."

She sighed again. "Adam." She laughed. "Would you look at yourself!"

I couldn't move well, but I managed to gaze at my arms and my stomach. I noticed I was naked, and everywhere my skin was withered and wrinkled. It was covered in purple and blue blisters that popped.

"Good Lord!" I yelled. It hurt to move, hurt to breathe. Everywhere my skin was black.

"You have to suffer this on your own."

I sighed and groaned again.

"Our plans can be fulfilled later. You know, my king —you may never heal completely."

"I don't want to heal at all," I answered. "I want to suffer, and then I want to die."

"You need to feed, Adam."

"Why the hell didn't you let me die?"

"Because I need you," she answered. "Because you are as my god now, Adam."

"Arrêter!" I yelled.

"I will not stop, Adam. I will not stop until you listen to me!"

"I don't care what you have to say!"

"You need to feed, Adam," she repeated harshly. "You need to feed so you can heal."

"I won't!" I yelled. "I refuse. Be angry. I don't care. Do what you wish to me. Beat me. Burn me. I don't care. I deserve it. I want it. I can never break away from you, Sekhmet. I feel myself changing. I am losing the Adam I used to know, the Adam I have finally grown to accept and understand. You're destroying me, Sekhmet!"

She didn't respond until I spoke again. "Please let me die!"

"Lying here this way will not kill you," she answered. "You will only be in a lot of pain for a long time. Don't you understand? That's the way it is with some of us. That's the way it is with you. You cannot die. Now get up and feed or lie here and heal slowly on your own."

"I don't believe you. I don't care how many times I have to try. I will take to the sunlight over and over again until I succeed!"

"You are hopeless, Adam. Hopeless because you are stubborn."

"I am not stubborn!"

"Every time you attempt to kill yourself, you will only be hurt. You were chosen to lead us, and after drinking from Verarsoe, Lacara, and now me as well, you cannot die. You are too strong. Now get the hell up or lie here and heal slowly. I'll leave you to it."

"I really can't die?"

"No," she yelled. "At least not by the sun, which is apparent. You're far too strong!"

I began to weep again. The blood tears ran into my wounds, and it hurt, but I wanted that pain. I deserved it.

"Oh good Lord, Adam," she yelled. "I need you. Now GET UP!"

"I WON'T!" I screamed.

She bit her wrist and pressed it to my lips. I tried to scream *no*, tried to pull away, but I couldn't. As soon as the blood started flowing, it was the most incredible feeling I had ever experienced. I felt like I was inside a dream where pain and fear didn't and never could exist. I could feel the wounds begin to close and heal. A comfortable numbness came over my body, and there was no more pain.

"There," she gasped angrily, pulling away from me. "Now it's still your choice. Get up and feed or lie here like a coward."

"I am not a coward!" I screamed so loudly I could have sworn I felt the earth shake.

I was still too weak to fight, but at least the pain had ceased. I would not surrender. I would lie here like this, naked and wounded.

I remembered crying out to her. I remembered wanting to know where I was. We were in a small room like an apartment. Sekhmet had killed the mortal family that lived there. But what about me? I was hungry too, and I *couldn't* get up. I remembered reaching out to her; I remembered dreaming of human blood.

She scolded me once again about my killing of Charlie. She told me I *didn't* understand. It wasn't my place to let him go; it wasn't my place to take him to Heaven. Perhaps she was right, but there was nothing that could make me believe what I had done was wrong.

Chapter Nine

I BEGAN LAUGHING as she turned up the volume on the tiny portable radio. People all over were raving about mysterious fires and the faceless, nameless suspects setting them. They were looking for an arsonist, not a vampire. I found it rather hilarious.

My mortal nature was depleting. I wasn't exactly the blue-eyed beauty I used to be; now I was the king of Sekhmet, a ruler of the undead. She had destroyed me—completely destroyed me.

I stood in the front room of a house where vampires lived before we destroyed them. The house was large, almost as large as my own back in California. I looked out the window, trying to find out where I was. The smell of the air, I knew. The feel of the breeze…everything was like something from a dream or a memory that had been lost and forgotten for centuries.

It was.

I fell to my knees. I felt the presence of the queen before she even entered the room.

"On your feet, Adam," she said, but she sounded kind and sorrowful.

"Why are we here?" I asked. "Why have you taken me back to a place of so much pain?"

She looked at me as if she didn't know what I was talking about, as if she had no idea where she had taken me, as if she had no knowledge of why I had kept this place as far from my memory as possible.

As soon as I smelled the air, I knew—she had taken me home. Sekhmet had taken me back to Switzerland, back to Geneva, the place I was at one time able to call my home. My memory haunted me with the faces of my past. Mary, Madeline, and my father's death along with my mother's all came flooding back to me, almost suffocating me.

I wept when I realized who had lived in this house—a family of four immortals, who lived how I lived, in a house with painted walls and shelves filled with books and diaries. They didn't deserve to die, so why had they? Oh yes, I remembered. I, Adam Gold, was the one Sekhmet had chosen. All others are useless until one of us says otherwise.

I looked at the mirror before my face, which I was ashamed to look into, for my wounds were not completely healed, and it shattered into tiny pieces. This made me smile, so I intentionally shattered every piece of glass in the house.

A ringing laugh suddenly startled me, and I turned to see Sekhmet. I smiled and met her embrace. I could feel the evil and the power pouring out of her, and I pulled away, coming back to myself for a moment. *What's happening to me?*

More were killed that night, and we moved on, traveling to other cities and countries, leaving my Switzerland behind. I still didn't know where we were most of the time, but it didn't matter.

I wanted to see my family. I wanted to know what they were thinking, what they were doing. Over the months that Sekhmet and I had been destroying, she had spared so few—the few she believed to either be the strongest, the ones I truly loved, and whom she believed would help her as I helped her.

For days, I thought of nothing but home. I wanted my family and my love. My Rayne, Clem, Relone, all of them. I even missed the expressionless, compassionless Victor who had cursed me with this life. I missed everything about California itself too. For days, I ignored Sekhmet. She killed while I slept, waiting to complete the healing.

She walked into the front room near dawn. "Your skin… It looks…human."

"It will pass," I answered. "It was the sun. It will pass. Please, my goddess…" I sighed and looked away from her for a moment. "Please. I want to go home. I want to see my family. I don't want to help you if it means I must leave those I love!"

"You are strong," she said, "but you love too much. You care too much of things that involve the heart. We are evil, Adam. Live it."

"I won't," I said quietly, as if speaking to myself. "I won't live without my family."

"You can see them if it is what you wish," she said, touching my face.

The feel of her skin sent chills through my body, and I almost fell limp against her. I felt tired; I felt lost. I wanted to fall asleep in her arms and let my limbs fall into the most natural and comfortable position while my head was rested against her breast. But she pushed me forward and looked deep into my eyes. I shuddered and tried to ask her what she meant. I couldn't speak. I wasn't breathing. She was overwhelming me with her touch, with her shimmering eyes staring into my own and her coal-black hair against my scarred skin. My limbs still hurt sometimes when she touched me with her strength. The sun's evil had scarred me, and I feared she was right, that I would never completely heal. My skin was browned, tanned like the flesh of a mortal. I didn't like it. I missed my pure white complexion, my vampire beauty. I wanted it back.

"You can see your family," she whispered through the darkness.

I tried to smile. "How?"

She touched my face again and smiled at me. "Do you think I gave you that medallion for nothing?"

"Can I...?"

She nodded.

I gripped the medallion in my hand and closed my eyes. At first, there was only darkness, but slowly, muffled voices found their way to my ears, and ghostly faces appeared before me. I waited for the images to become more clear, and I could see Rayne. I gazed around and saw Relone, Victor, and Lacara seated at a little, round table in Eric's home in London.

From another room came Clem. He'd been crying. As my vision became even clearer, I saw many I did not know. I recognized Verarsoe, but at least seven strangers stood beside the table.

Lacara spoke first. Her voice was muffled, but I could still detect her words. "Something must be done," she announced.

Rayne was silent, waiting for a reply.

"What can be done?" a dark-eyed creature beside Victor yelled.

"She must be destroyed," Lacara answered. "Our secrets will be released. We will all be exposed." She paused, sighing. "How can we even know Adam is alive?"

"He is," Relone declared.

Victor nodded. "He's mine. I know always where he is. I would know if he was dead."

I saw a look of contempt in Relone's eyes, but he said nothing.

The dark-eyed man continued. "If we pull together, we may have enough strength to bring down Sekhmet. Her plans will destroy all we have worked to create."

"No," Victor said softly. "I do not think it's possible."

"We cannot just do nothing," Lacara's voice boomed, making me shudder. "What can we do? Her power is beyond anything we possess."

"So we sit here and wait for our world to be destroyed?" the stranger said. "We wait for all we know to change around us, for our secrets to be scattered across the globe, directly into the hands of mortals?"

"No, Daniel," said Victor.

Daniel—as I thought. Oh how cold and frightened he looked.

More sighs and from Clem—more tears.

"What kind of power exists that can destroy her?" Rayne asked, almost as if she was frightened to speak. She spoke softly—slowly. Oh, Rayne, how I loved her. "Will Adam survive?"

"Sekhmet is using Adam as her tool. He is alive. I can feel it," Lacara answered. "But there is too much death to even count, too much evil coming from her. There must be a way, and if there is, I will find it. We will save our world, but first—we must save Adam!"

"Adam has a will of his own." Relone laughed. "Only he can save himself. Adam cannot be controlled by us. Not even you, Lacara, can pry him away from Sekhmet!"

Their words faded as the visions faded, and I released the medallion, seeing the face of The Mother before me again.

"Why do you weep?" she whispered.

I clung to her again, crying until I could cry no longer, and I told her I wanted to go home, that I missed my family, that this power was not deserved by me.

"I chose you because you have power, Adam, because you desire power, because I know you cannot refuse me. I have found the definition of our kind in you, and you have power! So much of it! You weep excessively!"

"You cannot make me like you," I whispered. "Look at me, Sekhmet. Do you see yourself?"

She looked at me as I told her to. "You don't want to rule beside me...?"

"You cannot use me," I answered. "It is only Adam Gold—Adam Gold who did not want the dark life, Adam

Gold who hates what he is. I am a young, miserable fiend with no desire to destroy!"

"Would you like to let your family know of our plans now? They will be the first to know. They will be our nameless loves, the ones who assist us. And those who oppose us will be destroyed."

I couldn't respond. I followed her through the night to London, where my family waited for a sudden rescue.

Chapter Ten

"YOU WILL RULE with us yet bow to us as well. If you refuse, we *will* destroy you. Do you choose power or death?"

Daniel looked frightened; he held Victor's hand and stared lovingly at the small child on his lap. Lacara spoke next.

"This cannot be done, Sekhmet!" she yelled. "It is a vile sin to destroy your own kind! You can already rule without killing!"

"Those creatures disgust me!" she shouted. "There is little or no blood from me that flows through their veins, and only I decide what is a sin, a crime! I hate them. All that will be in this newly formed world are those who are made of my blood, my children. All will bow to me and my king."

"It cannot be done!" Lacara yelled.

"I will destroy you before you tell me what I cannot do!" she screamed. "The only reason you are here is because you are strong. You are made from me."

She was lying. She loved Lacara, and she knew that. She loathed that love for her ancient child, detested that she felt the need to protect her from all harm.

She looked at me now. "And you, my Adam."

I moved my gaze to Relone and then down to the floor. I wouldn't look at her. I refused.

"Adam?"

"Look at him," Relone said, bringing my gaze back to him. "Look into his eyes. Do you not see fear? Fear, Sekhmet, anger and sadness. Not love. Not respect. You cannot change him. He is only Adam Gold. That is all he will ever be!"

"You swore to obey me!" she yelled, leaning toward me.

I looked at her now, trembling all over. "No. No, Sekhmet. *You* swore I would obey you. *You* told me I was your king and I would serve you as the others served me."

"I am the queen!" she said. "Why do you not believe in my power?"

"I believe in your power. I do not believe in my own. I cannot be the one to rule beside you. Nobody can. Don't you see? I was chosen to lead our kind into the new era, and that era is not meant to be one of terror, death, and destruction."

"How can you say this?" she demanded. "How can you say you choose how this world should be when I cannot?"

"Please," I pleaded. "Stop this madness, Sekhmet. Stop it!"

"I will not!" she yelled. "I will destroy you all!"

Fear slithered into me now. I had nothing I could say,

no words to argue, but I was the only one. It seemed everyone else had more to say.

"Then who will rule beside you?" Victor asked. "If you destroy us, you will be alone."

Her eyes now held a new look of fear—fear that perhaps this could be the beginning of the end of her reign. I looked at her almost with compassion but a hidden look of hate somewhere in my face. Her eyes were almost sad now.

She really was going to kill us. It was over now. We were all going to die.

My thoughts were interrupted by a strange tremble through the walls of the room. I looked to the others to make sure I wasn't the only one who sensed it. Everyone had a confused expression on their face. The shudder grew to a violent quaking, sending books and lamps crashing to the floor.

I made eye contact with Verarsoe, and he began sending me messages. The words "Satan's Own" came to my mind, and I saw Relone's face. What was he trying to tell me? Verarsoe smiled and nodded slowly. I shook my head, telling him I did not understand.

I was distracted when I felt Clem clutch the back of my chair. I stood and guided him into the now empty seat.

The shaking in the room had all of us either on the floor or clinging desperately to a piece of furniture. I held tightly to the back of the chair for support.

I thought for a moment I was hearing music, a beautiful, mystical sound. It occurred to me seconds later that I was hearing a heartbeat. The door flung open, and we all looked forward, startled and confused. A blinding light flooded the room. It was so bright it burned my eyes.

Clem howled, falling to the floor as blood streamed from his eyes.

Rayne and Relone were huddled together. Daniel was shielding the child in his arms, sheltering her from whatever was coming. Victor was staring at the floor, but he was shaking. The light slowly faded only enough to slightly ease the pain in my eyes. At last, it came into view—the most unimaginable creature in all the world; no human could comprehend it.

All of us were weeping from confusion now, and the beauty of this creature could bring anyone to tears, all but Sekhmet.

Verarsoe ran to the creature and dropped to his knees, bowing. "My Lord," he whispered, "I have kept your secret buried deep within my immortal soul!"

The word came to me like something from a dream, but I didn't speak it. Not yet.

The legends I had learned over the years in my life had all flooded back to me, and I thought hard about each and every one. It was as if my life was replaying in my mind. I could see myself on the ship, with Victor's teeth in my neck, the night when I first looked into that mirror as a vampire. I could see Elenore and Rayne; I could see Relone and Verarsoe. I could see all that had happened to me. My mind replayed the events of the shattered windows in the church and of the dying boy in the hospital—Charlie.

Please, Angel, don't let the doctors come back. Don't let them hurt me anymore. When you go back to Heaven, will you take me with you?

My life was going to end, wasn't it? The world I had known was over, and everything I had grown to understand was going to be stripped away. This angel that stood before us was nothing that any of us ever dreamed possible.

I am Adam Gold—vampire hero. I am a seducer of mortals yet immortals as well. I am a lover of the darkness, but suddenly, everything I have come to believe in and all I know and understand has slipped away, questioned, and forgotten.

I am a tormented creature, struggling to be the fearless blood hunter I am as I still try to attain humanity.

Verarsoe stood to his feet, and the other creature looked directly at me, which took my breath away. My body burned, and I was sweating. His ageless, stiff face was blinding to me. It hurt to look at him, but all the same, I couldn't take my eyes off him. He was surrounded in that light. He looked like an angel, and for fleeting moments at a time, I believed he was. I could not begin to describe him. I could not tell what color his hair was, his eyes, his skin. I didn't know then, and I do not know now. Too long had he lived for me to possibly understand. Too many centuries had he walked the earth. Too many eons had he spent hunting and creating. Too many wars had he seen, too many miracles occurring, mysteries solved, legends turned to myth and soon afterward forgotten. But he was only a vampire, wasn't he? I believed it was fair to say—he was the fault of my misery. After all, who else could there possibly be to blame now?

Clem was still on the floor, and I was becoming rather

worried about him. The majesty of this creature could bring the oldest, most powerful immortal to their knees. I stared at Verarsoe and back to the angel that stood before him. I heard the words, but his lips were still.

"You came back to me now, dark eyes—my child—my angel of the night?"

Only a beautiful smile from The King in return. I attempted to speak the name now, for everybody was thinking it. In a choked whisper, I tried to force the word from my lips—but nothing came out. I kept trying to speak but then realized I wasn't breathing, and I couldn't breathe. I didn't see much love from The King, or amazement either, which confused me even more. My beloved Clem was finally able to look at the creature with a little more ease, though his eyes were still bleeding. The pain seemed so worth it to gaze upon such beauty. Are we worthy to look upon this?

Verarsoe turned to us. "Here then," he started, "is the king of all immortals."

At last the word was spoken but not by me. It was Sekhmet who said it, and it should have been. She spoke it now with strength that caused me to stare at her, in awe of her power.

"Ké Hé Zule!" she cried. "Oh, my love!" She ran to him with open arms, and he accepted. He stroked her hair but for only a moment before pushing her forward harshly, staring hard into her eyes.

"You betrayed me!" he growled.

I knew he was not speaking English or any language I could define, and his lips were not moving, yet somehow, I understood every word.

"You dishonored yourself after I gave you a life of

darkness. You tried to destroy me. My sweet princess, did you not read the book?"

"The…book?"

"The book, my love. The secrets of destruction?"

She didn't respond.

"Only when the evil vanishes from the soul of the king may he die. Only when the lust for destruction, pain, and power leave the blood of The Father may he die. I had to forgive you, Sekhmet."

"How can it be?" she whispered. "I watched you burn."

He smiled. "No, my love. No."

We all looked away again until his smile faded.

I watched them speak through their minds to each other. The language was old; it wasn't English. I couldn't understand of what they were speaking, but it seemed affectionate, compassionate. And no, those sweet feelings between them did not comfort me. Sekhmet had found her king, and now she didn't need me anymore. The Father was back, and once more would he stand by his queen and reclaim his world.

There was more to it than that, for they seemed to be pleasantly debating. I was confused yet completely mesmerized. I was able to understand the words again when I tuned in. The story was of God and how he had cast The Father out from all of mankind and had cursed him with an evil life as a punishment for the striking of a vile pact with the devil himself, one that promised salvation after death and a seat of power within the very core of Hell. I wanted the truth. I knew God and Satan had nothing to do with this curse. Never had I ever longed for answers as much as I did then as I stared at those two angel-like creatures, immortal and clearly not much different than myself. I wondered how many secrets of Earth The Father had uncovered after living for so many long, lonely centuries.

He turned to us slowly and glanced at Sekhmet; she was crying. I wanted to ask her what reason she had to weep. I wanted to meet her embrace and share our blood between each other the way we had before, but I couldn't. The face of The Father stared blankly at us, and he pushed the queen in front of him, still grasping the back of her neck. I heard him whisper sweet words to her, words of comfort or some kind of consolation.

"Here then," he started, "is the queen."

What now? Who would die first? Who would be chosen to serve them, and who would be chosen to burn? He continued.

"And now I say farewell myself. Remember not these days of madness, my children, but remember the days of glory. Think upon the times when Ké Hé Zule and the Egyptian princess Sekhmet ruled the dark world as they were meant to. And remember also…if ever life becomes unbearable—there is always the rising sun."

I stopped breathing again. I didn't understand. Could it really be over? Was it possible that the source of all evil had come to stop evil?

I stared for a moment, waiting for his words to process in my mind, if words they had even been. Everything felt like a massive amount of unearthly sounds and feelings. None of it seemed real—but it was, and I knew it was. I was mesmerized—captivated. I couldn't move or breathe. I wonder what would have happened if I would have said something to him, asked him why or how.

Sekhmet was crying silently, clinging to him somehow—or I thought she was. It was hard to make out anything through that blinding light and the utter confusion. I couldn't look at the others, not even my Clem, who I was so worried about. All I could do was stare like a dumbfounded fool. For hours it seemed, I stood there looking at those ancient creatures.

Before I even knew he had moved, The Father had approached me. I felt like I was going to faint. I was crying though I didn't know it because I was still not breathing. He touched my face, and my entire body began to tremble. I could taste my blood tears in my mouth. I shuddered and closed my eyes for only a moment. It was so hard to look at him and even harder not to.

He spoke to me, but they were not words. Or I didn't think they were words. He told me, "When the evil has vanished from the soul of The Father may he die, and now I pass the leadership of this new era to you—Adam Gold. May you lead my kind—*our* kind into an era of peace. Never be afraid to love, Adam Gold. Never be afraid…to do good."

And with those last words, he was gone. I looked around for Sekhmet, but she was gone as well. They had gone away somewhere in the sands of Egypt to wait for the sun, where they would end together. I was unsure how I knew that, but I did.

We were finally free from the evil that almost destroyed our world, almost destroyed everything we had grown to love and understand, everything we cherished and held dear. The queen was gone, and I could have wept for her now—but I didn't.

Chapter Eleven

I STOOD UPON THE BALCONY, gazing out at the quiet greenery of Eric's back yard, the serene elegance of the silent night.

"My child," I heard. "You are strong."

I turned to see Verarsoe and smiled for an instant before embracing him. I was unsure why I had done so at the time. Perhaps it was because I prized his age, his power. Perhaps it was for comfort, or perhaps it was the love I felt for him, which I would deny. But I had held him tightly, and he didn't stop me but held me in return.

Daniel had left already with Victor, and all the other strangers had disappeared as well. Lacara remained, as did Relone, perhaps waiting for me. That made me wonder how long any of us would remain here in this life. I hoped I could be here for a long time more. Relone would be here; Relone would always be here. So would Verarsoe. It was me I was worried about—the potent Adam Gold.

How long will I remain before my life ends? I am on

my way into a new life now. This story had reason, had purpose, but there are other answers, other stories I have yet to tell—lost tales that have led to all that has happened, all the madness and the beauty.

"The medallion is gone, Adam," Verarsoe whispered as he pushed me forward. I thrust my hand to my chest and realized he was right, but I began laughing, and he joined in with me as we stood in each other's arms.

It was dark and still outside as I walked the streets. I could hear the clack of my heels echoing and my own breathing. I froze dead in my tracks when a strange tremble in the atmosphere alerted me, almost knocking me to my knees. I inhaled, preparing myself for what I knew I was about to encounter.

I turned around slowly with my eyes on her shoes. Finally, I looked up, and the air was sucked out of me. She was there, just as I remembered her, every detail as it had always been.

"My God—Madeline."

She smiled warmly and took a long stride forward, finding her way into my arms. I cradled her in my embrace like I had when she was just a child.

"Father," she whispered into my chest.

I pulled from the embrace to look into her eyes. "How…?" I couldn't find the words.

"Her name is Mona," she said.

"Her?"

"A woman. She found me many years ago. In all

honesty, Father, she should have killed me. I was reckless when I fed. Ruthless."

My memories assaulted me with the images of Madeline killing, almost ripping off her victims' heads.

"She taught me control. She has been with me all these years, masquerading as my mother so people do not ask too many questions. I felt it was time to finally see you again."

Tears moistened my eyes, and I pulled her into my arms once again.

Chapter Twelve

IT WAS a year later when I sat there on that bench, watching my mortal by passers. I loved the fact I wasn't hungry. Of course, it was typical that just as I wasn't hungry that a mortal approached me. He was one I would have chosen in a time of weakness when I couldn't have resisted him. He was golden in the hair; it was thick and soft. His eyes appeared mostly gray but shone blue in the light. He looked at me as if he knew I wanted nothing to do with him, as if he knew he meant less than nothing to me. He carried a heavy bag on his left shoulder, and without looking at me, he reached into the bag and handed me a book. It looked old. The cover was gone, and the entire thing was actually held together by Scotch tape and a rubber band. I smiled and silently laughed. I stood up to look at him, and he gasped, stumbling as he stepped back. I put my hand up.

"I'm not going to hurt you," I said.

"I know who you are. I know you very well. Even the accent is familiar to me."

I hadn't realized I had an accent; this time it was Italian. I had been thinking in Italian again. I looked at the book. The first page read, *Behind Blue Eyes.* And beneath it, *Adam Gold.*

I laughed. "I swear to you I do not wish to hurt you."

He nodded. "I know. I have read your autobiography about forty times. I don't need it anymore."

"A che cosi me serve?" I asked. "I wrote it, my mortal friend. What is it to me?"

"I...don't know," he answered. "I felt you had more of a right to it than I do."

"What do you want?" I asked. "Just get straight to it. Why are you here?"

"I am here because my sister..." He paused, still nervous and trembling a bit. "My sister, Emily, is seeking the dark gift. I was hoping you could help me stop her. Please do not take offense."

"Why would I take offense?" I asked. "I understand your reason for wanting to find me. Your reason is a good one. I will help you as much as I can. Thank you for the book, but really, William—I don't need it."

"You know my name?" he yelled.

"Oh." I laughed. "Forgive me." I touched his shoulder. "Do you know why your sister wants this?"

"I can guess," he answered. "We are all we have—each other. She is afraid of us losing each other. She wants to take the gift and give it to me. She doesn't understand I will never take it."

"Please do not lie to me, William. Who has she found?"

He lowered his head and whispered quietly, "Your child."

I froze. He hadn't realized I had heard him. Did he mean—could he mean—Madeline?

Dio Mio! Tradimento!

"She found him four days ago," he continued.

Him—Clement!

Emily stared motionless at the journal for a moment as her tears stained the pages.

"Please, Adam," she pleaded again, bringing her gaze back into my eyes. "Please don't tell me to keep him away. I love him."

"No," I answered. "You are in love with his beauty, ma chére. You and I both know that."

She wouldn't stop crying, and it was becoming a miserable sound. Her violet eyes were pouring her tears. I wanted to embrace her, to hold her close, to kiss her, but I couldn't.

I felt that eastern wind; I glanced that way, for the wind felt good against my newly healed flesh. She dropped her gaze back upon the journal and handed it to me. The light from the street lamp turned her blond hair into a ribbon of gold, and I couldn't take my eyes off her. Her tears glistened on her cheeks, and I wiped them away with my fingertips.

"I don't want it," she whispered. "Please—take it."

I weakly took the journal from her and ran my hand across the cover.

"I already know him." She reached into her purse and revealed a book. "I know you too. You can have it."

"Your brother already tried to offer it to me. I don't

want it, Emily. I really don't. I wrote it, ma amour. It is nothing to me."

"It shouldn't belong to me," she answered.

I smiled. "I wrote it for you. I wrote it for the outside world, as I write all my others."

She smiled. "Thank you."

"Goodbye, Emily."

"Adam Gold, don't you say goodbye!" she yelled. Her voice dropped to a whisper. "Please don't say goodbye."

I smiled. "Until tomorrow, Emily."

"I should never have done it to you, Clem," I said solemnly. "Dieu, I should never have done it to you!"

"I would have taken it," he answered. "If not by you, by someone else."

I smiled thinly and embraced him. "Dio ti benedico," I whispered.

He stared at me blankly.

"Bless you." I laughed. "God bless you, my child, my Clem."

"As always, Adam," he answered. "I don't know which way to go now. Really I don't."

"And I wish I could tell you, Clem. I've been there before." I turned my back to him. "Ghastly mistakes," I whispered, moving my hand to my lips. "So many ghastly mistakes."

He sighed. "I'm staying here," he whispered.

I turned to him and smiled.

"It wouldn't be right to return to Ireland."

"No," I answered. "No, it wouldn't, but what will your sisters want to do to me when they find out what I have done to *you*?"

He laughed. "Nothing. You think they don't know? They know, and they have known always that I wanted it." He sighed. "I think you should have kept a copy of your story."

"What is it to me?" I asked. "I wrote it. What good will it do me?"

"Remind you," he said. "Remind you of the changes you have brought to our kind by your ways."

"Perhaps." I smiled.

I left Moonlight Manor and walked slowly down the cul-de-sac. I met William at a café where I knew he would be, and as soon as he saw me, his eyes held a look of fear layered in anger.

"What have you done to Emily?" he growled.

"What she needed me to," I answered. "I said goodbye."

He sighed. "My father is waiting for us."

"Michael. His name was Michael, right?"

"How did you know that?" he asked.

I heard the terror in his voice. I pointed to the name on his brief case.

"Oh," he answered, calming a bit. "Yes—Michael Gardner."

I scolded myself for blurting out the name I had stolen from his thoughts and stared at my hands rested on the table.

"He loves her, doesn't he?" he asked.

I met his eyes again. "He does."

"Thank you for not giving her what she asks for. She has no idea what it is that she asks!"

"I know, which is why I will not give it to her."

He nodded. "Look, Adam, about that thing you said happened to you, was it…well…was it…?"

"True?" I laughed. "Yes, Will, it was true, though some of it may be fabricated or exaggerated, but you can make that judgment for yourself."

He smiled.

"I want to meet somebody," he said. "A certain character from your book. I was going to ask you if you had made him up or not."

"Of course I didn't. It is Relone, am I right?"

"Actually—no," he answered as if he was confused, surprised that I had guessed wrong.

"I like to refrain from prying into people's thoughts as much as possible."

"Oh, yes," he answered. "Of course. It is Victor, Adam," he said smiling. "I want to meet Victor."

"Victor?" I laughed. "Why Victor, mon cher?"

"You love him," he said with a laugh. "You love him, and there is so much of his life that is untold. If I knew his story…well…"

"You would publish it."

"Not without permission, of course," he answered, still laughing.

I smiled. "Then I think I have something you may like."

"No. I read your book, Adam. I know you found his journal. I'm tired of reading. I want to hear. I want to hear his story from his lips with the emotion, the tears, and the smiles. Please."

"I understand," I answered. "He has Daniel now and a small child, a beauty no doubt, but I don't know much about her."

"I would like to find out."

"I know, but will you know where to find them?"

"No, but perhaps the journal could help me with that part."

"Perhaps so. All right then."

"I've dreamed of it for so long!"

I laughed. "Slow down there." I held up my pocket watch. "Do you know what this is?"

"It's a watch, Adam."

"And do you know what it holds?"

"It holds…time, Adam."

"And he has all of it. Don't be too quick now, my friend. He is immortal. He has all the time in the world. Just be patient. Stop and think, William. Is this what you want?"

"It is. I have been thinking for a long time, Adam—a very long time."

"Yes, Will. All right."

Adam Gold 1991
    Je vous amour

About the Author

Sara J Bernhardt is an author and poet who has been writing since a very young age and is a winner of several poetry and short story contests. It is clear that Bernhardt writes in a realistic tone while still creating the enthralling feeling of fantasy. Her writing puts readers in a world that they will truly love to be a part of. Though the writing is edgy and catching it is also not too complex which makes it a comfortable and enjoyable read for everyone.

You can follow Sara at these locations:
Facebook
http://www.facebook.com/Sara-J-Bernhardt
Website
www.sjbernhardt.com

Other Works by Sara J. Bernhardt

https://books2read.com/HuntersTrilogySet

Summer's Deceit (Hunters Trilogy – Book 1): Jane Callahan is a reclusive, seventeen-year-old high school student dealing with the death of her beloved brother. Her home in Southern California with her mother is a constant reminder of her loss and pain. In hopes of escaping her past she moves to North Bend Oregon to live with her father, where she meets a beautiful boy named Aidan Summers. Jane is intrigued by his looks as well as his unusual ways of attempting to get her attention. After months of uncommon conversation and frustration, an uncertain romance brews between Jane and Aidan, but Aidan has a ghastly secret that could destroy everything.

Summer's Shadow (Hunters Trilogy – Book 2): Aidan Summers, a seventeen-year-old, stunningly beautiful genius, somehow finds his way into the life of Jane Callahan; a lovely girl trapped in soggy North Bend, Oregon.

In this new Tale by Sara J. Bernhardt, Aidan relates his side of the story. All of his dark secrets are revealed and all of his motivations behind his strange ways become known as the story unravels in a captivating narrative of suspense, romance, courage...and murder.

Summer's Redemption (Hunters Trilogy – Book 3): The secret alliance of The Silver Wing and the waging war with their evil rival, The Sevren, come into full view in a new light. The evil that still lurks and stirs behind the supposed destruction of The Sevren steps out of the shadows and spins a new tale of adventure, suspense, romance, mystery and terror.

Also from the Lavish family

Samantha Jacobey
https://www.lavishpublishing.com/authors/samantha-jacobey/

No one EVER had a summer romance like this!

When Charlie visited another plane parallel to our own, he discovered that Summer Angels and Dark Angels battle over the fate of man.

Faced with choices no one should ever have to make, his adventure has been fraught with twists and turns, with life and death hanging in the balance. His guardian, Clarisse, is the half that makes him whole, but sinister forces conspire to do more than simply keep them apart.

Find out if they can stand up to the powers that be in this thrilling magical adventure!!!

Rosinanti Series
Kevin J. Kessler
https://books2read.com/RosinantiSet

The Rosinanti Dragons are no more. Since their extinction nearly one thousand years ago these primal powerhouses have fallen into the obscurity of history's forgotten lore. In that time, humans have come to dominate the world of Terra, peacefully ignorant to one horrifying truth: ancient evil stirs around them, waiting to reclaim its lost world.

For Valentean Burai, animus warrior of the kingdom of Kackritta, the details surrounding humanity's victory over the Rosinanti are more than just a history lesson. The long-buried mysteries of this archaic conflict may hold the answers that he has so desperately sought regarding his own past.

As the awful truth of the Rosinanti's supposed demise comes to light, Valentean must stand together with Seraphina, a magically gifted princess, to embark upon a mission to maintain order and light throughout Terra. Only together can these two lifelong friends face down the resurgence of the Rosinanti legacy and combat the greatest threat their world has ever known.